10 MINUTE ADVENTURES

BEN 10

MIDNIGHT MADNESS

When you see these symbols:

Read aloud
Read the story together.

Read alone
Read the story by yourself.

Egmont is passionate about helping to preserve the world's ~~remaining~~ forests.
We only use paper ~~...~~

This book is made from pap~~...~~ ~~FSC®),~~
an organisation dedicated to p~~...~~ ~~sources.~~
For more information on th~~...~~ ~~out~~
Egmont's sustainable pa~~...~~

FSC
www.fsc.org
MIX
Paper from responsible sources
FSC® C018306

EGMONT
We bring stories to life

HOUGH

Grandpa Max had brought Ben and Gwen to the biggest shopping centre in the country. It even had a rollercoaster! But as they walked in, they saw some thieves being chased by security guards.

THIS PLACE HAS EVERYTHING!

HALT!

A HERO'S WORK IS NEVER DONE!

Ben slammed down the Omnitrix and turned into hairy, smelly Wildmutt to chase the thieves.

GROWL!

GROWL!

At a shopping centre, Ben, Gwen and Max see guards chasing some robbers. Ben turns into Wildmutt to catch them.

Wildmutt fought the thieves until they ran away. But the guards then chased after Wildmutt! He jumped into Max's Rustbucket to escape.

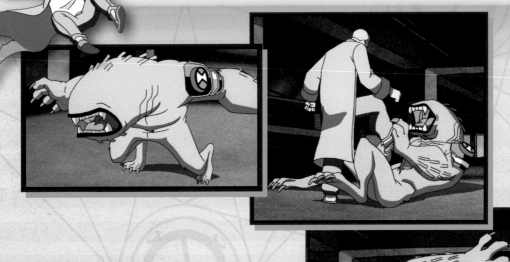

HE'S TRYING TO ESCAPE IN THAT CARAVAN. STOP HIM!

Inside the Rustbucket, Wildmutt turned back into Ben. The guards stopped the caravan, but they were very confused when they searched inside!

UH... LOOKING FOR SOMETHING, OFFICER?

Wildmutt fights the robbers, but then the guards chase him too! He jumps into the Rustbucket and turns back into Ben.

The next day, at the shopping centre, Ben took part in a hypnosis show hosted by a strange little man called Sublimino.

FOCUS ON THIS POCKET WATCH.

Using his pocket watch, Sublimino hypnotised Ben to make him think he was a crying baby, and then a clucking chicken!

CLUCK
CLUCK
CLUCK

CLUCK
CLUCK
CLUCK

A man called Sublimino uses his watch to put Ben in a trance. He makes Ben act like a baby, and then like a chicken!

7

Next, Sublimino told Ben to be an alien. Ben pressed down the Omnitrix, but Gwen pushed him behind a curtain before he transformed!

BEN, NO!

Ben turned into Grey Matter, but luckily, no one saw. Gwen sneaked him outside so Sublimino couldn't see the little alien.

YOU'RE RUINING THE PERFORMANCE!

COME ON, LET'S GO.

YOUR WILL IS MY COMMAND!

Then Sublimino tells Ben to be an alien! Ben turns into Grey Matter, but Gwen hides him before he is seen.

That night, Ben didn't sleep very well. The next morning, Ben, Gwen and Max went back to the shopping centre. Ben could hardly stay awake.

YOU OKAY, BEN?

JUST TIRED.

They soon learned that the rollercoaster's motor had been stolen. One of Diamondhead's crystals was found next to it! Max and Gwen glared at Ben.

WHAT? IT WASN'T ME!

That night, Ben sleeps badly. The next day, they learn about another theft. One of Diamondhead's crystals is found at the scene, but Ben says it wasn't him.

The next night, Gwen saw Ben sleepwalking! She and Max followed him as he went outside and pressed the Omnitrix.

BEN, WAKE UP!

In a trance, Ben transformed into Upgrade and sprang onto the roof of the shopping centre. The police began to chase him in their helicopters.

The next night, Gwen and Max follow Ben as he sleepwalks. He turns into Upgrade and the police chase him onto a roof.

The helicopters fired at Upgrade. He leapt onto the building's clock face and merged with it.

Upgrade used his power to turn the clock into a high-tech flying machine. Then he flew it up into the air to fight the helicopters! Gwen and Grandpa Max couldn't believe Ben had become a baddie!

TIME FLIES WHEN YOU GO ALIEN!

The helicopters fire at Upgrade. He jumps onto a big clock. Then he turns it into a flying machine and fights the helicopters!

Upgrade flew away with the clock and landed in an empty car park. Sublimino appeared from the shadows, looking for Diamondhead.

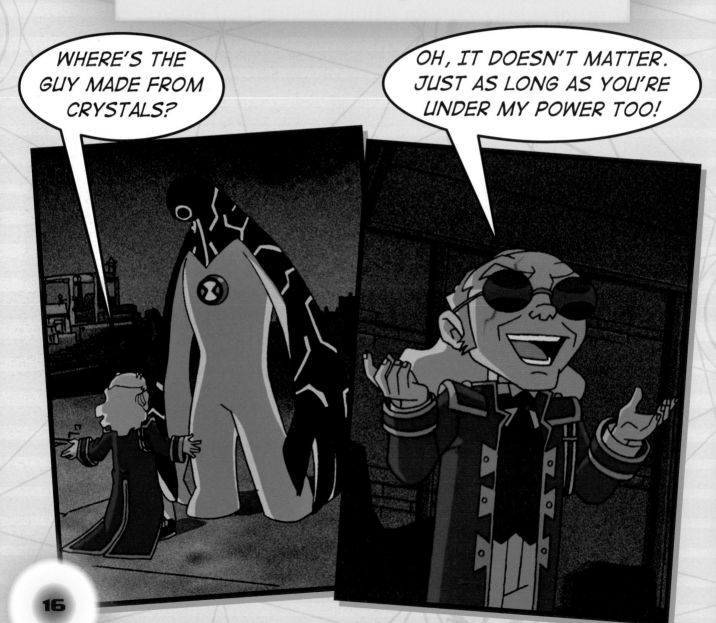

WHERE'S THE GUY MADE FROM CRYSTALS?

OH, IT DOESN'T MATTER. JUST AS LONG AS YOU'RE UNDER MY POWER TOO!

Sublimino took the clock and sent Upgrade away. So Upgrade turned a digger into a powerful tank and drove it back to the Rustbucket.

Upgrade takes the clock to Sublimino, who is controlling Ben when he sleeps! Then Sublimino sends Ben away.

In the morning, Ben woke up on top of the digger! But he had no idea how he got there. Something strange was happening to Ben at night. But what?

WHOA! OH, MAN ...

Late that night, Sublimino pressed a switch on his pocket watch. Suddenly, mysterious rays spread out from it.

AWAKE, MY SLAVES ... SERVE YOUR MASTER!

Ben wakes up outside, but doesn't know how he got there! That night, Sublimino turns on his strange pocket watch again.

The rays quickly hypnotised Ben again and he turned into Heatblast. Grandpa Max and Gwen chased after him to find out what was going on!

Heatblast flew to a warehouse and burnt a hole through the wall. Suddenly, other sleepwalkers arrived to steal the valuable goods inside.

In his sleep, Ben turns into Heatblast. He burns a hole in a wall to help other sleepwalkers steal things for Sublimino.

The next day, Ben was back to normal – but he was very, very tired! Gwen and Max worked out that Ben was under Sublimino's power when he slept. The villain was using Ben and other people to steal machine parts for him.

The gang had to stop him before someone got hurt! And until then, they had to keep Ben awake. He was too dangerous when he was asleep.

WE NEED TO FIND SUBLIMINO, FAST!

Gwen and Max work out that Sublimino is behind the thefts. The gang must stop him! Until then, Ben must stay awake.

The trio raced to the shopping centre. Suddenly, the stolen clock swung down from the ceiling, giving off strange rays. Sublimino appeared on all the TV screens and began speaking to the surprised shoppers.

YOU ARE FALLING INTO A DEEEEP SLEEEEP ...

The gang ran from the rays, but only Ben was quick enough to duck round a corner. Soon everyone was hypnotised, even Gwen and Max! Sublimino wasted no time giving them his evil orders.

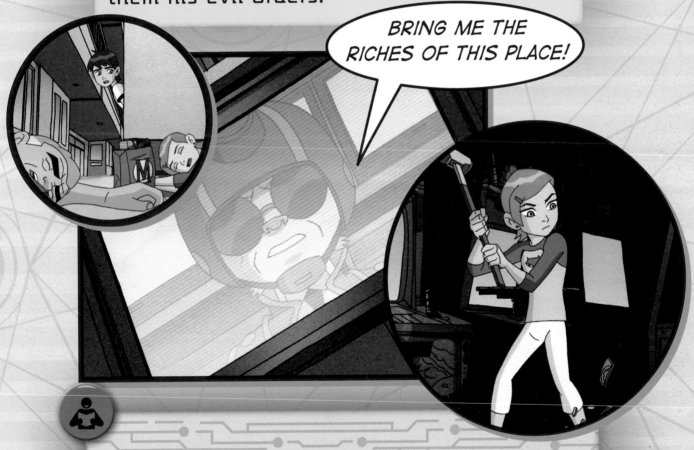

Sublimino hypnotises everyone in the shopping centre. He orders them to steal for him. Only Ben escapes the trance!

Ben knew what he had to do. He pressed the Omnitrix and turned into the plant alien, Wildvine! He swung himself up to the top floor to catch Sublimino in the security office.

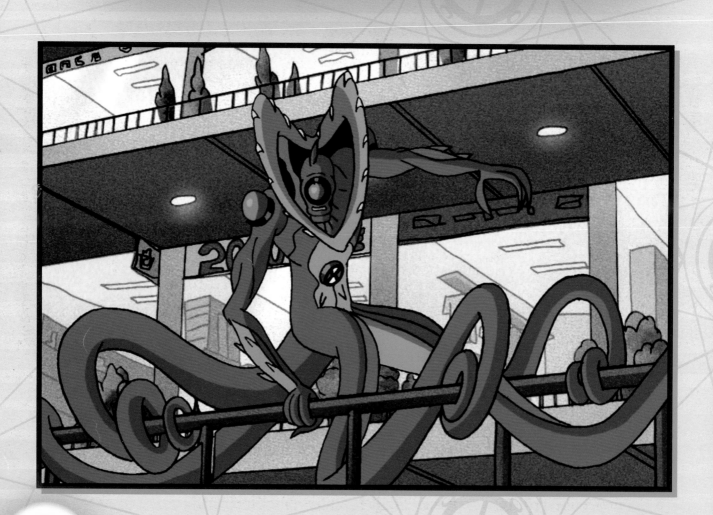

Wildvine wrapped his vines around Sublimino's ankles and dangled him high up in the air. Suddenly, the Omnitrix timed out and Wildvine found himself turning back into Ben ...

OH NO! BAD TIMING!

Ben turns into Wildvine to catch Sublimino. He dangles the baddie high in the air. But then Wildvine turns back into Ben!

Ben and Sublimino plunged through the air and landed on the hands of the huge clock! Sublimino tried to hypnotise Ben again, but Ben was able to swing past the villain and grab his pocket watch.

Ben pressed the button on the pocket watch to snap everyone out of the trance. Once again, the huge clock shot rays out across the room.

EVERYONE! WAKE UP! YOU'RE ALL FREE!

Ben and Sublimino fall onto the hands of the big clock! Ben grabs Sublimino's watch and stops the trance.

To Ben's relief, everyone woke up from the evil trance, including his family. But the rays made Sublimino lose his grip on the clock hand. He fell through the air ... and landed on a bouncy castle!

AAAAAAAAAAGGGGGGGGHHHHHHHHHHHHH!

Sublimino tried to escape, but was quickly captured by Max. Ben had saved the day once again, but he was so tired that he fell asleep on the clock!

LOOKS LIKE YOUR TIME IS UP, SUBLIMINO!

NICE JOB, BEN!

ER, BEN?

THE END

Everyone wakes from the trance. Sublimino falls off the clock and Max catches him. But Ben is so tired, he falls asleep!

Sign up today!

Monthly Catchup

children's books . mags . eBooks . apps

Does your child love books?

Register for Egmont's monthly e-newsletters and access our wonderful world of characters for **FREE!**

Catchup is packed with sneak previews of new books including much-loved favourites like Mr. Men, Thomas, Ben 10, Fireman Sam and loads more. Plus you'll get **special offers, competitions** and **freebies galore.**

SIGN UP TODAY FOR EXCITING NEWS STRAIGHT TO YOUR INBOX

Head to **egmont.co.uk** to register your details (at the top of the home page) and look out for *Catchup* in your inbox.

Get a whopping 35% off your first order! So you don't miss out on special offers, freebies and prize, add this email to your address book.

Monthly Catchup
children's books . mags . eBooks . apps

EGMONT

Hello,

You haven't heard from us in a while. It's not because we've forgotten all about you! We've just been working on some brand-new ways to keep you updated about our exciting books. Once a month you can look forward to recieving our newsletter: *Catchup.* It'll be jam-packed with really interesting stuff like, what we've been up to, sneak previews to new books including much-loved favourites like Mr. Men, Thomas, Ben 10 and Fireman Sam, as well as news about brand-new characters and books. You'll also get updates from our magazine team, special offers, competitions and freebies galore.

Stuff to do 'n' win

Signed *Mr. Tickle* to give away...

Thomas the Tank Engine

 **Zhu-niverse™ here we come!**
ZhuZhu Pets® have

Next month...

Sssh don't tell anyone but...

All About Bin Weevils Magazine Launching

All new special *Bin Weevils magazine,* on sale October 5th! It includes 7 amazing free gifts, comics, puzzles, posters, game tips and hints and a lot more.

All About Bin Weevils Magazine Launching

follow on Twitter | forward to a friend

So you don't miss out on special offers, freebies and prize, please add this email to your address book.

E1238